THE SURPRISE PARTY

PAT HUTCHINS

THE SURPRISE PARTY

ALADDIN PAPERBACKS

First Aladdin Paperbacks edition 1991

Copyright © 1969 by Patricia Hutchins

Aladdin Paperbacks
An imprint of Simon & Schuster Children's Publishing Division
1230 Avenue of the Americas
New York, NY 10020

Manufactured in China
20 19 18 17 16 15 14 13 12 11

Library of Congress CIP data is available.
ISBN 0-689-71543-9 (ISBN-13: 978-0-689-71543-3)
LC 91-10599

for MORGAN

"I'm having a party tomorrow," whispered Rabbit.
"It's a surprise."

"Rabbit is hoeing the parsley tomorrow," whispered Owl.
"It's a surprise."

"Rabbit is going to sea tomorrow," whispered Squirrel.
"It's a surprise."

"Rabbit is climbing a tree tomorrow," whispered Duck.
"It's a surprise."

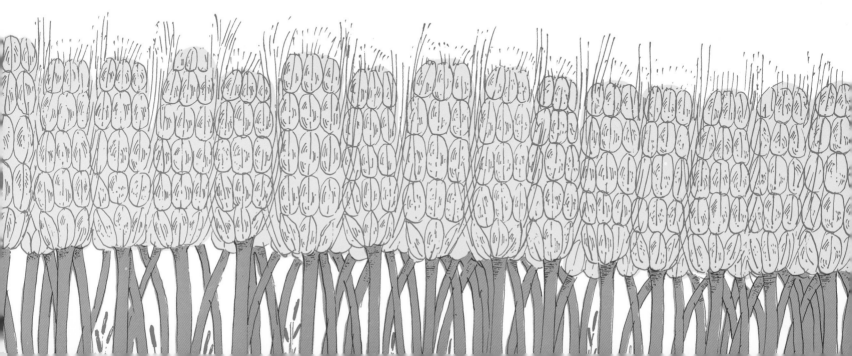

"Rabbit is riding a flea tomorrow," whispered Mouse.
"It's a surprise."

"Rabbit is raiding the poultry tomorrow," whispered Fox.
"It's a surprise."

"Reading poetry?" said Frog to himself.
"His own, I suppose. How dull."

The next day Rabbit went to see Frog.
"Come with me, Frog," he said.
"I have a surprise for you."

"No, thank you," said Frog.

"I know your poetry. It puts me to sleep."

And he hopped away.

So Rabbit went to see Fox.

"Come with me, Fox," he said.

"I have a surprise for you."

"No, thank you," said Fox.
"I don't want you raiding the poultry.
I'll get the blame."
And he ran off.

So Rabbit went to see Mouse.

"Come with me, Mouse," he said.

"I have a surprise for you."

"No, thank you," said Mouse.
"A rabbit riding a flea?
Even I am too big for that."
And Mouse scampered away.

So Rabbit went to see Duck.

"Come with me, Duck," he said.

"I have a surprise for you."

"No, thank you," said Duck.
"Squirrel told me you were climbing a tree.
Really, you're too old for that sort of thing."
And Duck waddled off.

So Rabbit went to see Squirrel.

"Come with me, Squirrel," he said.

"I have a surprise for you."

"No, thank you," said Squirrel.
"I know you're going to sea,
but good-byes make me sad."
And Squirrel ran up the tree.

So Rabbit went to see Owl.

"Owl," he said, "I don't know what YOU think I'm doing, but

I'M HAVING A PARTY."

And this time everyone heard clearly.

"A party!" they shouted. "Why didn't you say so?"
"A party! How nice!"

And it was a nice party.
And such a surprise.